THIS BOOK
BELONGS TO:

_____

Lucy and the Bear

A vivid memory
by Lucy Pope

Published in the United Kingdom by Jem Authors Agency
First Printed September 2022

Copyright © Lucy Pope 2022
Design by Jem Authors Agency
Front cover and original internal images by Mesha Kneen
Back cover image by Dawn Hann

A CIP record of this book is available from the British Library.

ISBN: 979-884-972-6328
www.jemauthorsagency.com

This book is dedicated first and foremost to my two grandsons, Harvey and Oliver.

I will forever love you, Big Nanna.

To my son Andrew, sister Eileen and two brothers Brian and Raymond, I hope you will read this book with joy in your hearts.

I would also like to dedicate this book to my friends, whom I consider family here at Birkin Lodge care home in Tunbridge Wells. Thank you for your friendship and kindness over the years Joyce, Barbara and Kalypso.

Lastly, I would like to thank my very special friend, Lizzie Penman-Green, not only for her friendship but I also thank the Lord daily for all her hard work and dedication in helping me write and publish this book.

Lucy and the Bear

One very chilly morning, Lucy got out of bed and
looked out of her bedroom window.

At the bottom of the garden, she saw something dark and mysterious underneath one of the bushes.

She was curious to find out what it was, so she dressed as quickly as she could, popped on her slippers and went outside to investigate.

Cautiously, Lucy made her way into the garden and slowly approached the dark shape hiding in the undergrowth.

As she got closer, Lucy stopped in her tracks.

It was a baby bear! In her garden! What was it doing there?

Lucy crept towards the little bear and slowly knelt down next to it.

Could she pick it up? Should she to stroke it?

She cautiously put out her hand and gently started to stroke its coarse dark hair.

The bear cub seemed to like being stroked and Lucy wondered what to do.

"Where is your mummy, I wonder?" Lucy said, more to herself than the bear, and began to look around the garden.

She was thinking about what she should do when her father called her to come inside.

Lucy reluctantly left the baby bear and ran back to the house to find her friend Peter there with his father. She had forgotten that Peter was staying for a sleepover that weekend.

Leaving their fathers talking, Lucy immediately dragged Peter outside. She was so excited to share her new friend with her old one, but Peter was confused as Lucy led him down the garden.

"What are you looking so pleased about?" he asked.

"There is a baby bear at the bottom of the garden," she said excitedly. "I've been feeding him some milk."

"I don't believe you," said Peter. "Bears don't live at the bottom of gardens."

"Well, see for yourself," Lucy said, pointing towards the little bear hiding in the undergrowth.

"I'm going to call him Charlie. Charlie, this is Peter. Peter, this is Charlie."

The bear looked up at Lucy lovingly. Peter could not believe his eyes. He had never seen a real bear before.

"Can I stroke him?" he asked nervously.

"Yes!" Lucy laughed. "He is very friendly."

Peter took a step forwards and Charlie bear lifted his head towards him. They were soon all happily playing and didn't notice the hours ticking by until Lucy's mum called them both in for tea.

"Wait here with Charlie," Lucy said, before running into her house.

She returned a few seconds later carrying the spare blanket from the bottom of her bed, which she used to wrap Charlie up snuggly and settle him down for the night.

When Lucy woke the next morning, she smiled as she remembered the dream about finding a little bear at the bottom of her garden. She was about to look out of her window when Peter suddenly burst into her room.

"You need to come and see this," he said, breathless.

Lucy realised it had not been a dream and excitedly ran out into the garden in her nightdress. When she caught up with Peter, she gasped as she saw Charlie with three other bears next to him.

Charlie looked like he had grown overnight and Lucy knew that she could no longer keep the bears a secret. There were just too many of them and they looked really hungry. She looked sadly at Peter, who seemed to understand, and the two children walked slowly back to the house to tell Lucy's mother.

Lucy's mother was astonished when she saw the four baby bears at the bottom of her garden.

"I'm going to call the other ones Freddie, Bouncer and Sid," Lucy said. "But first I think they need some food."

Lucy's mother agreed and decided to go and speak to the local vet to get some advice.

She left Lucy and Peter to play in the garden with the bears while her father kept a watchful eye from the kitchen window.

The bears continued to live with Lucy and her family for the next few days whilst the grown-ups decided what they should do.

On the fifth day, Lucy overheard her mother saying that her father must write to the authorities as the bears were getting too big and they obviously could not stay there forever. Lucy knew her parents were right but was very sad to hear this.

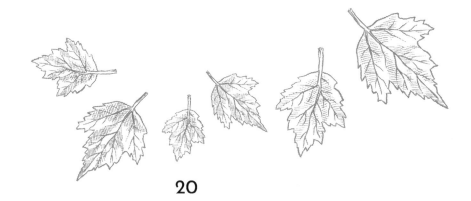

She went outside and noticed that Charlie seemed to be spending more time by one particular tree. Lucy went to investigate and discovered that this was because there was yet another bear!

This one was a little girl cub who must have been hiding all this time. Lucy decided to call her Sylvia.

Over the next few days, lots of people came to visit Lucy's house. Some were friends or family wanting to see the cubs and others were from the local authority deciding what to do with them.

They all agreed the garden was too small for the bears and that they needed to live in an appropriate environment to help them grow and thrive.

One day a kindly-looking lady wearing big glasses walked down to the bottom of the garden where Lucy was playing with Charlie and Sylvia.

"Lucy," the lady said, "we've come to a decision about the bears. We are going to build them a really big enclosure at the zoo where they'll have lots of room to play."

Lucy smiled, but still a little tear formed in the corner of her eye.

"And we've all agreed that the names you gave them will be the bears' official names."

Lucy looked at Charlie and stroked his head as he ate a raw potato. But she couldn't hold back the tears of sadness.

The bears stayed with Lucy until their new enclosure was ready for them at the zoo. It was a full-time job to look after them and make sure that they had enough fish, meat, fruit and vegetables, but Lucy could not have been happier.

When the day came for the bears to move to the zoo, she felt very sad but she was happy that they had a wonderful new home to go to. Lucy went with the bears to help them settle in.

She was overjoyed when she saw that each bear had their very own tree house with lots of things to climb and more food than you could shake a stick at.

Freddie, Bouncer and Sid ran off to explore, and Sylvia chased after them, but Charlie clung to Lucy's leg and wouldn't let go. He seemed very sad about his new home, but then Lucy had an idea to make him feel happier.

She climbed into Charlie's enclosure and coaxed
him with an apple to try his new tree house.

When he climbed up, he found Sylvia was already in there. He was instantly happier when he realised he would be sharing his tree house with her.

Lucy stayed with Charlie and Sylvia for hours until all the bears were settled and happy enough to enjoy their new surroundings.

When it was time for Lucy to leave, she kissed all of them lovingly on the forehead and waved goodbye with tears in her eyes even though she knew she would see them again the next day when she came to visit.

To this day Lucy still visits the zoo as often as she can to see her best friends, Charlie and Sylvia, and their own little family of cubs. And Freddie, Bouncer and Sid, of course!

The End

Printed in Great Britain
by Amazon

85893731R00023